PIG the STAR

PHOTO SHOOT
CALL SHEET

ON SET: 9:00 am

STAR #1: Pig (Pug)

STAR #2: ~~Trevor (Dachshund)~~

PIG PIG
PIG PIG.

For that lovely cast back in '99.
I'm just so sorry . . .

First published in Australia in 2017 by Scholastic Press, an imprint of Scholastic Australia Pty Ltd.

This book is a work of fiction. Names, characters, places, and incidents are either the product of the author's imagination or are used fictitiously, and any resemblance to actual persons, living or dead, business establishments, events, or locales is entirely coincidental.

No part of this publication may be reproduced, stored in a retrieval system, or transmitted in any form or by any means, electronic, mechanical, photocopying, recording, or otherwise, without written permission of the publisher. For information regarding permission, write to Scholastic Inc., Attention: Permissions Department, 557 Broadway, New York, NY 10012.

ISBN 978-1-338-31575-2

The publisher does not have any control over and does not assume any responsibility for author or third-party websites or their content.

12 11 10 9 8 7 6 5 4 3 2 1   18 19 20 21 22 23

Printed in the U.S.A.   169

Originally published in hardcover by Scholastic Press, April 2018

This edition first printing, September 2018

The artwork in this book is acrylic (with pens and pencils) on watercolor paper.
The type was set in Adobe Caslon.

PIG the STAR

Aaron Blabey

SCHOLASTIC INC.

Pig was a pug
and I'm sorry to say,
he just LOVED attention.
He'd show off all day.

He'd shout, "LOOK AT ME!
I'm the BEST!
I'm a STAR!"

But then came the day
that he took it too far . . .

Yes, Trevor and Pig
had a big photo shoot.

They wore little costumes.

They looked really cute.

"Isn't this fun?" giggled Trevor with glee.

But Pig pushed right past him
and yelled,

"LOOK
AT
ME!"

"Aren't I just fabulous?

Aren't I divine?

Now back off, Salami!
These costumes are

MINE!"

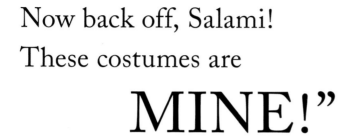

Yes, Pig ruled the photos.

He hogged every shot.

He whispered to Trevor,
"I'm IN and you're not."

And under the lights
as the camera went SNAP,
Pig felt like a rock star . . .

. . . and started to RAP–

"YO!

I'm a star, y'all!

Yeah, dog–
I'm the BEST!

Now, get me a donut,
you sausage-shaped pest!"

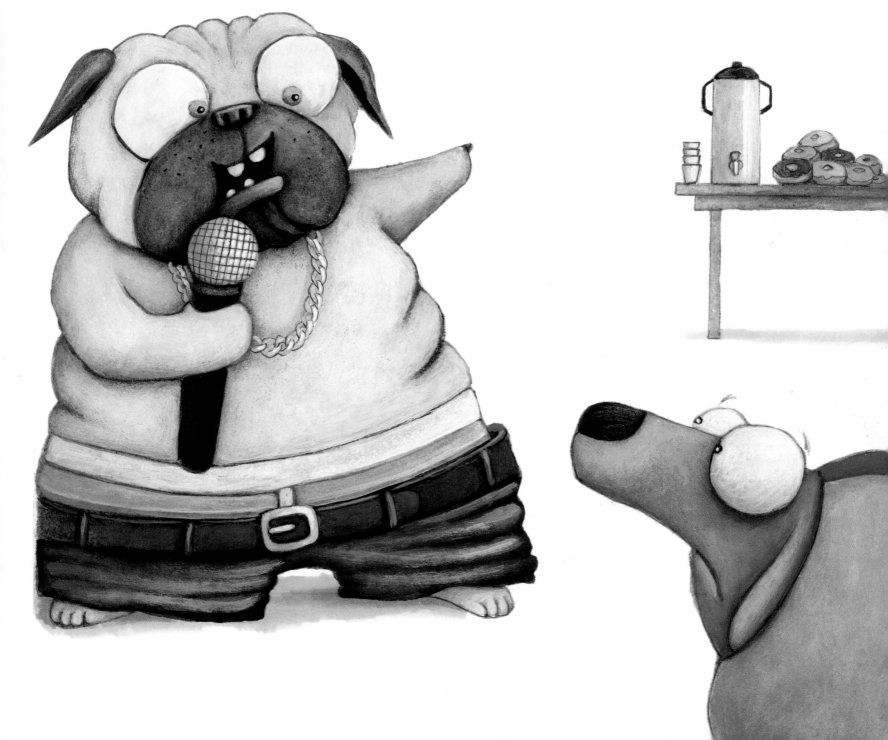

But then something happened
that changed the whole shoot.
The man with the camera said . . .

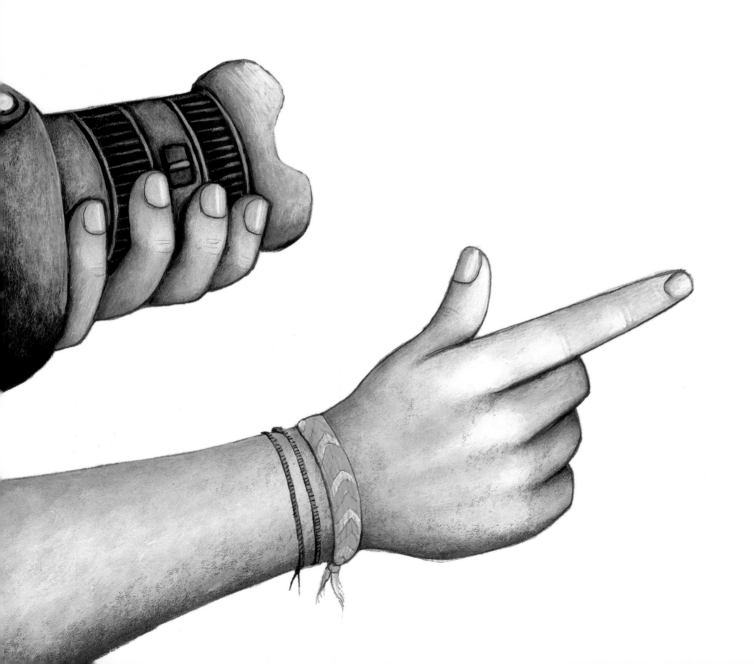

"That dog is CUTE!"

"Wow, Trevor's a STAR!"
the photographer said.

Pig couldn't believe it!

And then he saw RED.

He shrieked,

"I'M
THE
STAR!"

and he knocked Trevor flat!

SPACE PUPPY

But Trev bumped his rocket . . .

and the rocket went . . .

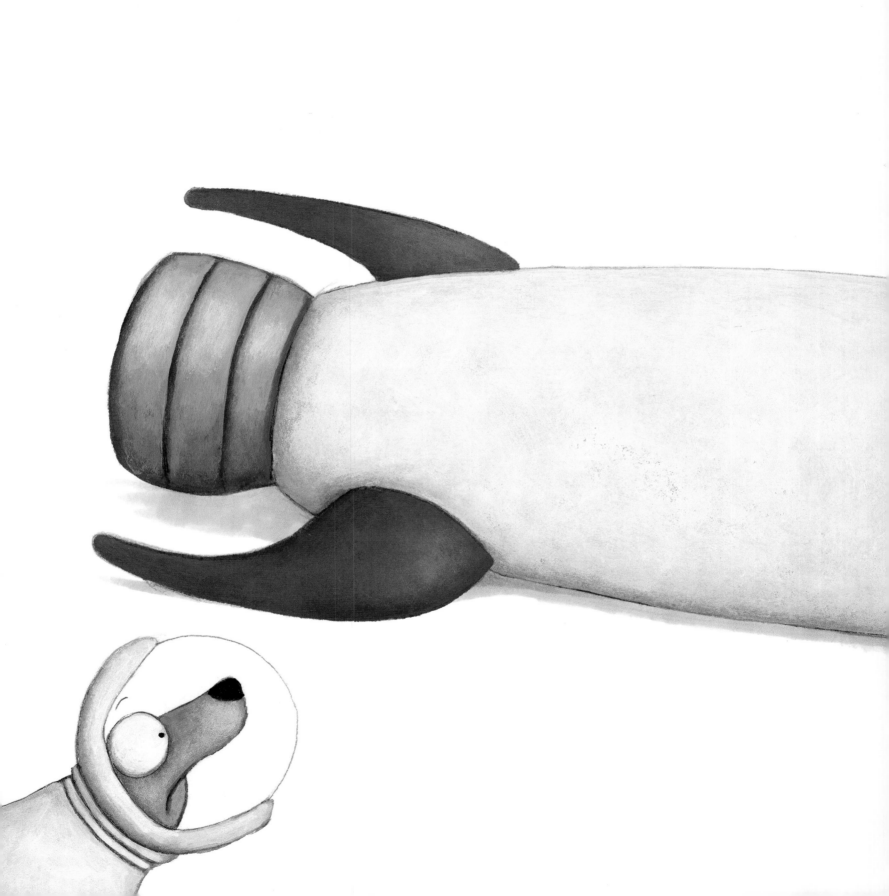

. . . SPLAT!

These days it's different,
I'm happy to say.
Pig's dreadful antics
have all gone away.

He's not such a show-off.
He's not such a swine.
And although it annoys him . . .

He lets Trevor shine.